D0296009

A Moment for Joe

Also by Diana Hendry

FIONA FINDS HER TONGUE
THE NOT-ANYWHERE HOUSE
THE RAINBOW WATCHERS
THE CAREY STREET CAT
A CAMEL CALLED APRIL
(Blackbirds)

MIDNIGHT PIRATE
HETTY'S FIRST FLING
SAM STICKS AND DELILAH
(Redwings)

A Moment for Joe

Diana Hendry

Illustrated by
Duncan Birmingham

Julia MacRae Books
A division of Walker Books

For Sophie Green

First published in Great Britain 1990 by
Julia MacRae Books
A division of Walker Books Ltd
87 Vauxhall Walk
London SE11 5HJ

British Library Cataloguing in Publication Data
Hendry, Diana *1941–*
A moment for Joe
I. Title II. Series
823′.914[J]

ISBN 0–86203–440–X

Typeset by Graphicraft Typesetters Ltd Hong Kong
Printed and bound in Great Britain by
BPCC Hazell Books Ltd Aylesbury

Chapter 1

Joe Dash was the odd one out in his family. His mother, his father and his sister, Lydia, all looked alike – they were dark and skinny and they were always in a hurry. But Joe was fair and plump – and slow.

Everyone in the Dash family was very busy. Mr Dash was always dashing off to a Very Important

Meeting. Mrs Dash had a morning job at the doctor's and an afternoon job at the dentist's and so she was always 'in a dash'. And Lydia, who was thirteen, was the most dashing Dash of all. Lydia belonged to the choir and the guides. She was a member of the Swimming Club, the Tennis Club and the Drama Club. She had a Saturday morning job at the greengrocer's and on a Sunday morning she went dashing off on her bicycle to do her newspaper round. Lydia never had a moment to spare and nor did anyone else in the Dash family. Except Joe.

Joe had a lot of moments. On a summer morning he would wake up to find a patch of sunlight on the floor of his room. He liked to sit in it and suck his thumb and wake up slowly and warmly.

He had a 'moment' at breakfast time when he looked out of the kitchen window and watched the grey squirrels leaping up the tree. And he had quite a long 'moment' cleaning his teeth and pulling faces at himself in the mirror. In the

winter he had lots of ‘moments’ which he spent lying on his tummy in front of the fire.

Joe didn’t like to rush and hurry and dash. Joe liked to dilly and dally. He liked to dawdle and drowse. He liked to dream and doze. But there was always someone saying, “Hurry up Joe!” or “Get a move on Joe!” Joe’s teacher said, “You’ve got the wrong name, Joe. You should be called Joe Slow not Joe Dash.”

It was impossible to tell any of the others about his moments – about the puddle of sunlight, the squirrel in the tree and the pictures he saw in the fire – because they were all in too much of a hurry to listen.

Even Joe's teacher was in a hurry. She bustled along as if she had a train to catch and couldn't be stopped, and when Joe *did* try to stop her to ask a question, she held up her hand like a traffic policeman and said, "Not now, Joe, I'm in a hurry."

There was only one member of the Dash family who was slow, like Joe, and that was Uncle Worthington. Uncle Worthington, however, lived in London and Joe rarely saw him. He had been to visit once when Joe was very small. Joe remembered him as large and bald – and yes, slow. Uncle Worthington had wandered about the house in his bare feet, wearing a silky dressing gown (with a red dragon on the back) until it was almost lunch time. Then he had stretched and yawned and said he thought it was time to start the day.

Mrs Dash who had started *her* day hours ago, had said sharply,

"It's the early bird that catches the worm you know, Uncle Worthington." And Uncle Worthington had said, "But I'm not a bird, Clara dear, and I've no wish to catch worms – very nasty creatures. Why don't you sit down and have a nice cup of tea with me?"

"You've already had five," said Mrs Dash, "and I've better things to do than sit about drinking tea."

Joe remembered that Uncle Worthington was never in a hurry and that he always had plenty of time to talk and play and he never put up his hand like a traffic policeman and said, "Not now, Joe."

And so Joe was very pleased

when one morning at breakfast Mrs Dash opened a letter and said, "It's from Uncle Worthington. He's coming to stay."

Lydia groaned. She was eating a piece of toast and putting on her coat at the same time. (Lydia held the family record for dressing,

eating her breakfast and being on her way to school all in the space of five minutes.) "He's such a slow coach," complained Lydia. "He takes hours eating a meal and hours having a bath and we all have to wait around for him."

"Well, I'm not waiting around for anyone this morning, " said Mr Dash. He looked at his watch and tutted. "I'm ten minutes late for the office already. I'll have to dash." And off he went. He was in such a hurry that he only had time to blow them each a kiss from the front door. They heard his car roar out of the garage like a tiger let out of its cage.

"I'm off too," said Lydia and Mrs Dash and Joe heard Lydia's feet running down the path.

"Get a move on, Joe," said Mrs Dash as she said every morning. "I must be at work in ten minutes."

"When's Uncle Worthington coming?" asked Joe.

"Monday," said his mother. "And goodness knows what we'll do with him. He's slow as a tortoise. Slow as a snail. I just can't get on with things when he's sitting around. Why I've known him take three hours over his breakfast!"

Joe thought that a breakfast that took three hours sounded wonderful! (Next to dillying and dallying, Joe liked eating.) Imagine *not* having to gulp your cornflakes, *not* having to leave half a mug of milk because there wasn't time for more. Just imagine sitting in your dressing gown, eating a tower of toast and watching the grey squirrels going up and down the tree until it was almost time for lunch! Just imagine no-one saying, "Hurry up, Joe!"

There was only one thing Joe wished would hurry up – the days between now and Monday when Uncle Worthington was coming.

Chapter 2

It was a good job that Uncle Worthington chose to arrive on a Monday because the Dash family were not quite so fast on a Monday as they were on a Friday. They got faster as the week went on so that by Saturday they were all going at the speed of a hurricane. If they were cars, you would say that on

Sundays they went at thirty miles an hour, on Mondays forty miles an hour and by Saturday they were going at a hundred miles an hour.

Uncle Worthington was late of course – that was a part of being slow – and they all had to wait for their supper.

"Ah! Cottage pie!" said Uncle Worthington. "What a beautiful sight is a cottage pie. Its top looks like the roof of a barn covered in snow."

They all gazed at the cottage pie impatiently while Uncle Worthington went on about its beauty and the warm things – like carrots and mince – waiting underneath the roof of crispy snow.

"Perhaps we can eat now?" said Mr Dash tapping his knife on the edge of the table and looking at his watch.

"Grace first," said Uncle Worthington and they all had to put down their knives and forks.

"Which one shall we have? 'For what we are about to receive'? That's a bit dull. I shall make one up." Uncle Worthington closed his eyes for what seemed like hours and then he said,

"*Thank you Lord for cottage pie,*
Thank you Lord for flowers and sky,
Thank you Lord for a baby's cry,
Thank you Lord for you and I,

Thank you Lord for tears and sighs . . ."

"And for letting us eat our cottage pie!" Mr Dash finished.

"Ah yes," said Uncle Worthington, opening his eyes, "I was almost forgetting the cottage pie."

Uncle Worthington was still only half-way through his cottage pie when everyone else had finished theirs, and when it came to pudding, he ate one spoonful in the time it took Lydia to gobble ten.

Uncle Worthington liked to pause in between mouthfuls and talk. The Dash family were not used to talking at meal times. They ate as fast as they could and then hurried off to whatever they were doing next.

"I'm sorry, Uncle Worthington," said Lydia, "but I can't wait any longer. It's choir practice night."

After supper Uncle Worthington put on his slippers, got out his pipe and sat down by the fire. Everyone else dashed off. Lydia to choir, Mrs Dash to a meeting of the Parent-Teacher Association and Mr Dash to the garage to chop logs. Only Joe was left.

"Time to sit and think," said Uncle Worthington, "that's what I like." Smoke-rings rose from his pipe like misty thoughts.

"Do you ever look at pictures in the fire?" asked Joe.

"Often," said Uncle Worthington. "I've seen strange caves and underground palaces in the fire."

"Sometimes there's a lump of coal that looks just like a cat," said Joe.

"Or an elephant," said Uncle Worthington.

"I've never seen an elephant," said Joe.

"You have to be very patient," said Uncle Worthington.

In the morning Lydia had to batter on the bathroom door and ask Uncle Worthington to hurry up.

Uncle Worthington popped his face (covered in shaving cream) round the door. "Time waits for no man," said Uncle Worthington, "but when I am shaving, dear Lydia, *you* are going to wait for me." And wait Lydia did, until Uncle Worthington had shaved *and* polished his bald head.

Uncle Worthington came down to breakfast in his dressing gown with the red dragon on the back.

("He should have a tortoise on the back of his dressing gown not a dragon," Mrs Dash whispered to Mr Dash.)

Mr Dash finished his porridge in a great hurry and went off to chop a few more logs before going to work.

"You sit down and have a cup of tea with me, dear," said Uncle Worthington to Mrs Dash. "You're always on the go."

Mrs Dash, who drank her tea standing up at the sink while she washed the dishes, was shocked by this idea.

"I can't stop now!" she said. "There's the beds to be made and the shopping to be done and I've got to be down at the doctor's for half-past nine."

"I'd have a cup of tea with you,

Uncle – only I've got to go to school," said Joe.

"We'll have a long slow cup of tea when you come home," said Uncle Worthington.

"If there's time," said Mrs Dash. "Joe has his homework to do and his piano practice and he should help his father with the logs."

"What is this world if full of care, we have no time to stand and stare?" asked Uncle Worthington.

But Mrs Dash wasn't used to poetry at breakfast time and she whisked away Uncle Worthington's tea before he could have a second cup.

When Joe came home from school, he found Uncle Worthington sitting on the wall at the bottom of the street, puffing thoughts out of his pipe.

"What are you doing here?" cried Joe. "Have you been locked out?"

(He wondered if Lydia might have done this – accidentally-on-purpose.)

"I'm watching the world go by, old chap," said Uncle Worthington.

Joe liked the way Uncle

Worthington called him 'old chap', it made him feel grown up.

"Oh!" said Joe, very surprised, for nobody in his family had ever had time for this.

"Want to join me?" asked Uncle Worthington.

So Joe jumped up on the wall by

Uncle Worthington and they watched the world go by and it was very interesting indeed. They saw Mrs Atkinson with her twins, Jenny and Penny; they saw Tom Miller skateboarding home from school, and Mr Roberts feeding his cat on the windowsill, and Adam Patterson

going to collect the evening newspapers which he delivered to all the houses on his bicycle.

"Is this having time to stand and stare?" asked Joe.

"It is indeed, old chap," said Uncle Worthington. And then they both went home and had a long, slow cup of tea and Mrs Dash hustled and bustled about them and told them both to hurry up because she wanted to lay the table for supper.

By Friday all the Dash family (except Joe) were very fed up with Uncle Worthington.

"He takes an age in the bathroom," said Lydia.

"He takes forever over his breakfast," said Mrs Dash.

"He talks so slowly," said Mr Dash (for he liked brief sentences, chopped up like logs), "he's got no full stops."

"I wish he'd hurry up and go," said Lydia.

Only Joe hoped that Uncle Worthington's visit would be long – and yes, SLOW.

Chapter 3

Uncle Worthington was still there on Saturday. He thought that because Mr Dash didn't have to go to work and Lydia and Joe didn't have to go to school, everyone would slow down. But they didn't.

That Saturday afternoon the Dash family were going at Full Speed. They crammed into

Saturday all the things they didn't have time to do the rest of the week.

Mr Dash went out into the garden and chopped twice as many logs. Then he stacked the logs up with their pale sawn edges all facing outwards like rows and rows of round faces.

Mr Dash liked doing two things at once, so every now and again he ran into the house to make a telephone call and then he ran out again to do some more chopping. It was dial, ding, chop, chop, dial, ding, chop, chop, all morning.

Mrs Dash was baking. She was baking three cakes, two pies, one tray of biscuits and a syrup sponge and no-one dared go into the kitchen in case they got hit by a high-speed flying rolling-pin.

Lydia was doing her homework and the ironing at the same time. She would iron the sleeve of a blouse and then dash over to the table, write a sentence of a story and then rush back to iron the second sleeve.

"It's like Paddington Station

here," said Uncle Worthington who was sitting on the sofa reading the newspaper – slowly. "Or Piccadilly Circus."

"We don't have time to sit around in *this* family," said Mrs Dash.

"What's wrong with sitting around?" asked Uncle Worthington. But Mrs Dash didn't know the answer to this so she pretended not to hear and began beating eggs and sugar together very loudly (and quickly) with a wooden spoon.

And then all of a sudden the sitting room did turn into a sort of circus. The telephone rang. Mrs Dash, with her bowl of sugar and eggs still in her hands, rushed to answer it. Lydia was half-way between the ironing board and the table. Mr Dash had dashed in from the garden holding a log. They all collided in the middle of the floor. It was a Dash Crash!

With a big sigh Uncle Worthington rose slowly from the sofa, climbed over the Dash family and answered the telephone.

"It's the wrong number!" he said.

And then they all laughed and Uncle Worthington said, "Now let's take things nice and slowly," and he sent Joe for a bandage for Mr Dash's toe (because he'd dropped the log on it) and he scraped up the eggs and sugar that were soaking into the carpet and he rubbed Lydia's head where she'd bumped it. And then he made a big pot of

tea and toasted some crumpets and they all SAT AROUND and drank tea – SLOWLY.

Mrs Dash said, "This is really rather nice." And then, "Now that I've got time to look at you properly, Joe, you need a hair cut." And Joe, who hated having his hair cut, wondered if it was *always* a good idea to have time to stand (or sit) and stare.

Uncle Worthington felt very pleased with himself indeed. He felt like a Christian missionary who had converted a tribe of savages. He thought he had changed the Dash family into a Slow family. But he was wrong!

Chapter 4

In the second week of Uncle Worthington's visit, a letter arrived for him. It had been forwarded by his neighbour and its post-mark was a week old. "I found this letter when I was watering your plants," wrote Uncle Worthington's neighbour, "and as it looks rather important, I thought I'd send it on."

The letter said:

Dear Mr Worthington,

You will be very pleased to hear that you have won a prize in our competition. The prize is a fortnight's holiday in Spain. Unless we hear otherwise, we shall expect you to be at London airport, ready for your flight to Barcelona, at 11 am on October 1st.

Yours faithfully,

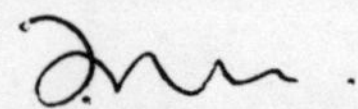

The Dash family were very impressed when they heard about Uncle Worthington's prize. "What did you have to do to win?" asked Lydia.

"I had to write a four-line rhyme about those little Spanish oranges – satsumas," said Uncle

Worthington. "I was sitting over breakfast one day ..." (the Dash family exchanged looks – sitting about, they thought) "... when this rhyme came to me. Out of the blue you might say. Or perhaps out of the orange!"

"What was it?" asked Joe.

"It was this," said Uncle Worthington, and he stood up and recited his rhyme:

"*Spanish satsumas are super and*
sweet,
I'm gloomy without a satsuma to eat,
I'd sooner satsumas than apples
or pears,
With a room of satsumas I'd lose
all my cares."

Joe was just about to ask for a repeat of this when Mr Dash stood up waving the letter and shouting, "It's today! It's today!"

"What's today?" asked Uncle Worthington rather crossly because he wanted to recite his rhyme again.

"The holiday in Spain! The flight's at eleven o'clock. It's today, Wednesday, the first of October!"

All the Dash family leapt to their feet.

"Hurry up, Uncle Worthington!" cried Lydia.

"It's two hours to the airport. I'll take time off work to drive you there," said Mr Dash.

"No time for breakfast," said Mrs Dash.

Even Joe joined in. "You'd better get dressed at once," he said.

Uncle Worthington looked at them all in horror and went quite pale.

"I can't possibly go!" he said. "Not in such a hurry. Not in such a dash. It takes me an hour just *thinking* about getting up in the morning before I can actually do it. I need a week to think about a holiday in Spain."

"Nonsense!" said Mr Dash. "You can't miss a holiday like this. Look, it says here – the chance of a lifetime. I'll get the car out."

"It's no good, I haven't got my passport," said Uncle Worthington hopefully sinking into a chair.

"We'll collect it on the way to the airport," said Mr Dash. "Now look snappy!"

Uncle Worthington looked horrified.

"It's a good job it's half-term," said Lydia, "we'll help you pack."

"I'll have to have a bath first and choose some books and I need to iron my holiday shorts," said Uncle Worthington in a flap and a panic.

"No time for any of that," said Mr Dash briskly.

Uncle Worthington had never moved so fast in his whole life. He

was allowed a two-minute shower and a cup of tea – standing up. Lydia and Joe packed all his clothes in double quick time. Mr Dash had the car door open for him.

Joe sat in the back seat of the

car with Uncle Worthington and held his hand because Uncle Worthington said he felt as if he was flying before he got on the aeroplane, and off they rushed. They stopped at Uncle Worthington's house and Lydia ran like greased lightning up the stairs and grabbed Uncle Worthington's passport from the top right-hand drawer of his desk and then off they zoomed to the airport.

They made it just in time. Uncle Worthington was the last passenger to check in.

"You can have a lovely slow holiday," said Mrs Dash.

"Maybe that's what we all

need," said Mr Dash, "a long slow holiday."

"Well," said Uncle Worthington who was smiling now and thinking of sunshine and satsumas, "maybe there are times when you need to hurry – times when you need to make a Dash for it!"

He walked through to the departure lounge. "I'll come and tell you all about it," he called back to them. "Slowly!"

Joe waved and waved until the plane was far away in the sky. When it was high up the plane looked as if it was moving very slowly although he knew it was going very fast.

"It was nice having Uncle Worthington around," said Lydia when they got home. "Sort of relaxing."

"Tomorrow I'm going to sit on the wall and watch the world go by," said Joe.

"It sounds a nice idea," said Mrs Dash, "but right now I'm late with the lunch. Hurry up and lay the table for me."

"Let him be," said Mr Dash. "Let's have a moment's peace and quiet."

That was a moment they all shared.